The
Adirondack
Kids®#12

The Pond Hockey Challenge

By Justin & Gary VanRiper
Illustrations by Carol VanRiper

Adirondack Kids Press, Ltd.
Camden, New York

The Adirondack Kids® #12
The Pond Hockey Challenge

Justin & Gary VanRiper
Copyright © 2012. All rights reserved.

First Paperback Edition, May 2012

Cover illustration by Susan Loeffler
Illustrated by Carol McCurn VanRiper

Published by
Adirondack Kids Press, Ltd.
39 Second Street
Camden, New York 13316
www.adirondackkids.com

Printed in the United States of America
by Patterson Printing, Michigan

ISBN 978-0-9826250-2-6

In Memory

Robert Douglas "Scott" Stuart III
"Uncle Scott"
1939 to 2012
"Lover of all things Adirondack"

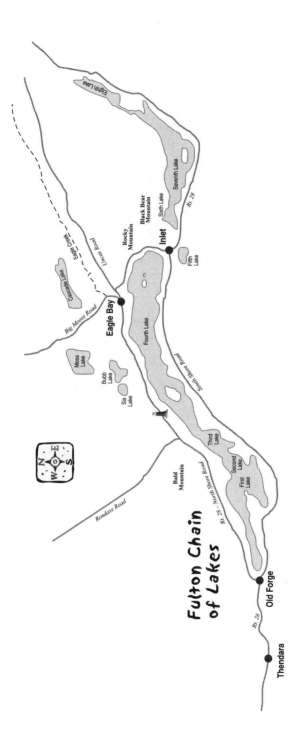

Fulton Chain
of Lakes

Contents

Dax reached the puck first and slid with
her captured prey across the width of the rink!

from Chapter 15 – Checked Out

Chapter One

Let it Snow

Justin Robert was hoping for a white Christmas. And he was getting one. The temperature in the Adirondack hamlet of Inlet was the lowest it had been throughout December in years, and fluffy snowflakes the size of quarters were beginning to make their lazy decent to the frozen ground. Cars passing by were sweeping them off the busy highway – but it was easy to see the branches of the Christmas tree across the street in front of the Town Hall becoming fringed with the white of winter.

"Do you think it's true?" Justin asked his best friend, Nick Barnes, who was busy attempting to capture one of the large wet flakes in his wide-open mouth.

Nick smiled as one of the flakes appeared to be landing near the tip of his tongue. He followed it until his eyes were nearly crossed, and frowned as the flake changed direction with all the swiftness of a drifting autumn leaf. "Do I think what is true?" he said, and opened his mouth to try for another one.

Justin removed his blue bucket hat, which was becoming caked with the freshly fallen snow, and shook it. "About these snowflakes," he said. "Do you think it's true that every single one of them is different?"

"How can anybody know for sure without checking each one?" It was Jackie Salsberry, Justin's other best friend. And she was bounding down the steps of her favorite gift shop, swinging a colorful, holiday bag.

"We thought you were going to take forever," Nick said.

"There's only one shopping day left," Jackie said. She lifted the bag. "I had to find something just right for Mom and Dad."

"I always make something for my mother at school," Nick said. "And my father likes it when I make him a card." He grinned. "My mom told me he still has every one I've ever made."

Justin was excited. "I can't wait until my parents see what I have for them," he said. "I found the perfect present this summer."

It had been a hard secret for Justin to keep for so long. He was afraid his mother and father might find the surprise, so he kept changing the hiding place. He almost forgot to bring it with him to camp, but thanks to his cat, Dax, he remembered. The last place Justin had hidden the gift was in a corner behind her litter box. It had been a very safe hiding place since it was his job – and his job alone – to clean the box. And that was his final chore before the family piled backpacks and packages into the Jeep to head north.

Jackie turned to him. "I am so glad your parents changed your cabin into a four-season camp this fall," she said. "We finally get to spend a whole Christmas vacation all together."

Justin could not remember when her smile was brighter.

"Hey, there, Miss Jackie Salsberry." A tall boy with dark hair and darker eyes brushed by Justin and Nick and walked right up to her, invading her personal space.

"Hello, Braedon," Jackie said. She took a small step away from him. "What brings you to our humble little town of Inlet?"

Justin recognized that tone from his friend. It was Jackie's, be-very-careful-what-you-say-to-me-next voice.

The tall boy ignored her question and looked back over his shoulder down at Justin and Nick. "Don't tell me these two are on your team," he said.

Jackie gave him an icy stare. "Yes, they are," she said.

The boy shook his head as he walked away with a wry grin. "You promised us competition," he said. "Maybe you should look that word up in a dictionary."

Jackie turned back to her friends and sighed. "Those boys have no idea what they are in for," she said.

The confrontation made Nick forget that his feet were getting numb from standing on the cold sidewalk so long. "What team?" he said.

"He was looking right at us," Justin said. "What competition?"

Before Jackie could answer them, the plate glass window of the gift shop shattered from the inside out, shards of glass scattering onto the glazed sidewalk and into the street.

Chapter Two

The Challenge

"It was a deer?" Justin's mother handed her son and his two friends each a cup of hot chocolate. A small plate of fresh and frosted Christmas cookies was set on a coffee table between them. The smell of baked butter and vanilla still lingered in the air. "Well, you all remember the poor doe that felt trapped in Kalil's grocery store in the summer," she said. "It was probably only a matter of time before something like this happened. I hope no one was hurt."

"Thank you for the cocoa and cookies, Mrs. Robert," Jackie said. "We were the closest ones to the window when it happened, and we're all fine."

"Mr. Newman didn't look fine when he came running out of his store," Nick said. "Who wants air-conditioning this time of year?"

Justin cradled his steaming cup in both hands to get his fingers warm. "Not only that, Mom," he said. "It was a white deer. All white."

Nick nodded, and selected a cookie – one shaped like a loon. "That's right," he said, and dipped the loon's beak into his cup. "That deer was as white as the marshmallows here in my chocolate. And it had antlers."

Justin's father stoked the logs in the open fireplace around which they all were gathered in chairs and on pillows on the floor. "An albino deer would be quite rare," he said, and poked at the glowing logs once more. There were some snaps and crackles and a burst of new flames. "Are you sure the deer didn't have any dark patches or spots anywhere on its body?"

"It sure looked all white to us," Justin said.

"Albino?" Nick said. "Is that a country where white deer come from?"

"No," Jackie said. "Albino is just what you call a deer, or any animal, that is born missing its normal colors." She moved her pillow to sit closer to the warmth of the fire. "That deer was really lucky, too. Two cars just missed it."

"Blizzard," Justin said.

"It started snowing again?" Nick said. He jumped up and cheered. "Let's go make a snowman!"

"I'm not talking about the weather," Justin said. "That's my name for the white deer. I'm calling him, Blizzard."

A disappointed Nick sat back down and took another loon cookie.

Justin couldn't stop rehearsing the near tragic scene in his mind. The whole incident still seemed to him a blur. The window smashing. The cars swerving. The powerful, white animal darting across the highway and disappearing behind the town's lighted tree and into the falling snow.

"You three enjoy the fire," Mrs. Robert said. She nodded at her husband. "Mr. Robert and I have a few things to finish in the den."

Justin's eyes brightened and he smiled. "Do you mean like wrap some presents?" he said.

"Never mind," Mrs. Robert said, and smiled back at him. She turned to Jackie before leaving the room. "Now might be a good time to tell them."

Justin was startled by his mother's parting remark. It was like a million things raced through his mind all at once. *Tell us what? Was Jackie moving?* That was the first thought that came to his mind, and the worst thought of all.

"It's about Braedon," Jackie said.

Justin was relieved. "Do you mean the boy we met in town?" he said.

"What did he do?" Nick said, and frowned. "He wasn't mean to you in school, was he? Bullying is not allowed at our school at all."

Jackie laughed. "He's not a bully," she said. "And he doesn't go to school here in Inlet. He goes to Old Forge. He was just talking about our hockey game."

Nick's frown remained. "What do you mean by *our* hockey game?" he said.

Justin studied Jackie's face and suddenly he wasn't relieved anymore. "Was that why he asked if we were your teammates?" he said.

Jackie shifted uneasily on her pillow. "Okay," she said. "Let me tell you what happened."

7

Nick groaned. "I knew it," he said. "We're doomed."

"It's not a big deal," Jackie said. "We were on a school field trip in Lake Placid with some of the classes from Old Forge. When we all visited the rink where the United States won the Olympic Gold Medal in hockey, some of the boys from Old Forge said they had the best hockey players in the Adirondacks. I told them that Inlet had some good players, too." She stopped and took a quick sip of chocolate. "Then one of the boys said, 'Prove it.'"

"And so you challenged them to a hockey game?" Justin said.

Jackie nodded. "No," she said. "They challenged me. And since there is no one else in my school this year my age, and I knew both of you would be here for Christmas vacation, I accepted their challenge."

Nick nearly spilled his hot chocolate as he rolled off his pillow and around on the floor as if he was in pain. "We're double-doomed," he said.

"But we're from Eagle Bay," Justin blurted. He was sure he had come up with a brilliant reason why he and Nick were not qualified to play on her team.

Jackie smiled. "If you and Nick lived at your camps all year, you would go with me to the Inlet Common School," she said. "Both of you more than qualify."

Nick was still moaning. "That boy, Braedon, had arms that were bigger around than my whole neck," he said.

Justin sat with his mouth open. His blank stare

was interrupted only by an occasional blink.

Jackie was becoming annoyed. "Will you two stop it?" she said. "The game will be fun. I have one other friend for our team who will also be visiting this week." She stood up and reached for her jacket, now toasty warm from the fire. "Come on, I'll show you where we're going to play."

"I've seen the rink in Inlet before," Justin said. "Besides, my mom and dad won't let me walk all the way back to town now. It's Christmas Eve."

"And I still have to make a card for my dad," Nick said. He stuck two cookies together and crammed the treat into his pocket. "A frosting sandwich for later," he said, and grinned.

Jackie picked up her shopping bag and handed Justin his coat and bucket hat. "We're not going back to Inlet," she said. "I have a surprise for both of you down at the lake by the docks."

Chapter Three

The Rink

Snow was falling again and accumulating quickly now. If it weren't for the rocky shoreline, it would have been nearly impossible to tell where the covered lawn ended and the ice on the lake began. Dusk was also fast approaching, making it even more of a challenge for the three bundled-up friends to see very far ahead. They could hear at least two snowmobiles racing somewhere out across the invisible landscape so they knew they were headed in the right direction.

"Here it is," Jackie said, carefully stepping over the rocks and onto the ice. "Our official skating rink for the pond hockey challenge."

"The ice must be pretty thick for snowmobiles to be on it," Justin said.

Jackie nodded. "Some places on the lake are never safe," she said, and used her scarf as a wrap to help cover her ears. "It's been so cold for so long that it's already a foot thick here where we'll be playing."

Nick remained on shore and was more interested in the brand new white stuff at his feet. "This snow is sticky," he said. "It should be perfect for a snow-man." He packed a small snowball and began to roll it across the ground. "Let's make a big one right now. I'll do the bottom."

Justin was captivated with the homemade rink, located between the Robert's and Barnes' family docks. It was impressive enough to him that he could feel his heart beat a little faster. "There are walls and everything," he said. He pointed through the falling snow toward a large shadow located near the center of the rink. "That's way too big to be a snowmobile," he said. "Is it someone's car?"

Jackie laughed. "Not quite," she said. "It's a zamboni."

Nick stopped rolling his snowball. "Zamboni?" he said. "That is a country, right?"

Jackie sighed. "Actually, Zamboni is the name of the man who invented the machine that helps keep the ice on skating rinks nice and smooth," she said. "Come on, I'll it show you."

Justin's eyes lit up. "Oh, I saw one of those with my dad a long time ago at a hockey game in Glens Falls," he said. Moving with Jackie toward the middle of the rink for a closer look, he was surprised. "But this sure isn't the way I remembered it."

Nick temporarily gave up on his snowman. After a running start over the rocks and onto the rink, he stopped suddenly, purposely causing his boots to plow through the snow as he slid the final few feet over and next to his friends.

Before them sat a blue tractor with a shovel in front, and rugged rear wheels that were almost as tall as they were. Hitched behind was a small trailer that was dragging a sharp metal blade and carrying what appeared to be a barrel of water.

"This ice resurfacer isn't as fancy as the kind they use at the professional hockey arenas," Jackie said, hands on her hips. "My father borrowed it to help make our rink. It's one they use to make the rinks every year for the *Adirondack Ice Bowl,* and it does the job!" She turned to her hockey recruits. "So – what do you think? You're on my team now, right?"

Justin had to admit he was warming up to the idea. He really liked the rink, and had always enjoyed roller blading back at home. But at first he didn't dare say a word. He knew if he slipped and even said the word 'maybe' out loud, Jackie would take that to mean, 'yes'! Instead, he found himself offering another excuse. "But we don't even have any equipment," he said.

Justin's comment actually encouraged Jackie, because he had not said that he would not play. "You can wear what you have on right now," she said. "Snow pants, a jacket, mittens …"

"What about skates?" Justin said.

"You can rent them in town," Jackie said. "And helmets, too."

"Hockey sticks?" Justin said.

"We have plenty of sticks at my house," Jackie said. "So, you'll even have choices." She smiled.

"And some of the ones I have are multi-colored and look very cool."

She really is convincing, Justin thought. *It's like she's thought of everything.*

"But I've never skated before in my whole life," Nick said.

Ah, Justin thought, and it was back to reality. *She had thought of everything except that!*

Jackie went on undaunted. "You'll catch on quick," she reassured Nick. "Listen. There's no body checking, and if you do check someone, you have to sit out of the game for good."

"Body checking?" Nick said. "What would you even check someone for in a hockey game – a fishing license?"

Justin was beginning to enjoy this. It was going to be tough to convince Nick to play.

"Checking is when you bump into another player on purpose to knock them over to stop them," Jackie said.

"So, it's like no bullying is allowed," Nick said. It was obvious from his expression and tone he really liked that idea.

Jackie nodded. "Kind of like that," she said. "And there are no slap shots, which means you can't smack the puck really hard, and you're not even allowed to hit the puck with your stick above your waist."

Nick stood politely shaking his head. "It all sounds like it's pretty safe," he said. "But there's still one problem."

Jackie sighed. "What is it?" she said.

"I've never skated before in my whole life!" Nick said, even louder than he said it the first time. "I would just keep falling down."

"How do you know that if you've never even tried it before?" Jackie said.

For once Nick was at a loss for words.

"You could be our goalie," Justin said, not believing he was actually joining Jackie in trying to persuade his friend to play. "Goalies just stand around in one place."

Nick's eyes grew wide. "Sure," he said. "They just stand around with everybody shooting pucks at them!"

"There's no goalie," Jackie said.

Justin and Nick both looked puzzled.

"Do you see the small wood boxes at each end of the rink?" Jackie said. "Well, they're almost covered up with snow now."

Justin and Nick nodded.

"Those are the goals," Jackie said. "Each team has four players and your team tries to shoot the puck into one of the open slots in the front of the box. There's no goalie. In fact, you aren't allowed to hang out in front of the goal at all. This isn't like the professional hockey that they play in the Olympics." She looked directly at Nick and paused to drive home her point. "This is pond hockey."

"You're not even playing on a pond," Nick said. "It's a lake."

"Call it lake hockey if you want to," Jackie said. "I'm asking you both again. We'll be playing right here the day after Christmas at noon. Are we a team?"

"I vote, yes," Justin said. "I'll try it."

"Traitor," Nick said.

"Nick!" Jackie said. "Will you be on our team?"

"Blizzard," Nick said.

"Stop trying to change the subject," Jackie said. "It's been snowing hard for nearly half an hour now."

Nick frowned. "No, I mean Justin's Blizzard," he said, and pointed just beyond the west end of the rink, to a spot near the end of the Robert's dock.

Justin turned and squinted his eyes, thinking it would help him see more clearly through the falling snow. It didn't help at all. "Do you see him, Jackie?" he said.

"I do now," Jackie said. She pointed along with Nick. "There."

Justin suddenly caught the young buck's movement, which appeared to him to be deliberate and slow. "It is Blizzard," Justin said, and started his way toward the end of the dock. "And I think he's hurt!"

Justin felt a THWACK on his back.
A snowball had successfully hit its mark.

Chapter Four

Blizzard!

"Stop, Justin," Jackie said. "Where are you going?"

"I just want a closer look," Justin said, as he inched his way out further toward the animal. He felt a *thwack* on his back, and turned to see a red-faced Nick still standing next to Jackie. A snowball from him had successfully hit its mark.

"We can't do anything to help that deer even if he is hurt," Nick said. "Come back or I'll get you again." He was already kneeling and gathering snow in his mittens to reload.

Justin ignored them both and kept moving forward, stepping over the rink's short plastic wall and further out on the lake. But now everything had again become a blanket of pure white. "Thanks a lot, Nick," he called back. "Blizzard's gone." He stopped and looked down toward his boots.

Jackie and Nick shuffled past the zamboni, being careful not to slip and fall. When they reached Justin, he was still peering down at his feet.

"What is it?" Nick said.

"I see them," Jackie said.

"See what?" Nick asked. "Justin's boots? Can't we go back to the camp and look at them inside where it's warm?"

Jackie ignored him. "They're Blizzard's tracks, and they're filling up fast," she said. "You could be right, Justin. That deer might be hurt. It looks like one leg could be dragging."

"I knew it," Justin said. His shoulders dropped. "But Nick is right, too."

"I am?" Nick said. He grinned. Then he stopped grinning. "I'm right about what?"

Justin lifted his head and peered into the blank landscape. His face was filled with sadness.

Jackie answered for their friend. "Justin means you were right there is nothing we could do for the deer right now, anyway," she said.

Nick hated seeing the pained look on his best friend's face. "But remember how you got us all to help save the loonies and the lost pelican in the summer?" he said. "You can't save every single animal and bird that's in trouble on the whole planet."

"Nick is right," Jackie said.

"I am?" Nick said. This time he grinned and didn't stop grinning.

Jackie placed her hand on Justin's shoulder. "We don't even know how bad Blizzard is hurt," she said. "And he may not be hurt at all."

"Let's go home, Justin," Nick said. "It's Christmas Eve."

"Yes," Jackie said. She held up her holiday bag.

"I still have to get home and wrap these presents."

"And I want to get my candy cane off the tree at our camp," Nick said. "We got some this year that are weird colors and flavors."

The more Nick and Jackie talked about Christmas, the more Justin's mood changed to match that of his friends. "Well, maybe," he said.

"That's a maybe," Nick said.

"And a maybe is yes," Jackie said. "Follow me."

"Where are you going?" Nick said. "I thought you said we were going home."

"We are," Jackie said. "Let's go."

"But the camp is this way," Nick said.

Justin shook his head. "You're both wrong," he said. "I should know where my camp is. It's this way."

The three huddled back together as the snow from above filled their tracks below and closed in on them from all sides.

"We're lost, aren't we?" Nick said.

"Maybe," Justin said.

"Oh, no. I know what that means," Nick said, weakly. "We're doom —"

Jackie placed her mitten over his mouth. "Don't you dare say it," she said.

But they all knew, miracle that it was, even three times in one day, Nick was right again.

Chapter Five

An Ice Surprise

Nick was moaning. "I should never have pointed to that deer," he said. "If I hadn't, we'd already be home."

"Shhh," Jackie said. "Let's listen. We can't see very far, but maybe we'll hear some noise that will tell us which way to go."

They stood motionless in a circle of silence, the falling snow slowly swallowing up their boots and little puffs of condensation like smoke signals exiting their panicked mouths.

Justin whispered, "Did you hear that?" he said.

Jackie nodded. "Snowmobiles," she said.

"This way," Justin said. He began to move away from the sounds they heard. "We'll keep the snowmobiles behind us."

"I don't think so," Jackie said. "We should walk toward them."

"Then, let's vote," Justin said.

Nick exploded. "Just tell me which way to walk," he said, the volume of his voice rising with each spoken word. "My feet are getting cold, and I want to go home!"

The snow was deep enough that the footing was secure, but now it would be even more difficult to tell when they were finally off the lake.

"We can't just stand here all night," Justin said. "Our camp isn't that far away."

"You're right," Jackie said. "It isn't that far away – unless you move in the wrong direction."

"All right," Nick said. "I vote we go Justin's way." And he began marching.

The three friends locked arms to avoid becoming separated, and it wasn't long before they all began to question Justin's sense of direction.

"This sure seems like a long way," Nick said.

"That's because we're moving a lot slower," Justin said. But silently he agreed with Nick. "Wait, did you hear that? There's a snowmobile again."

"Yes, I heard it," Jackie said. "And it sure sounds like it's a lot further away than when we heard it the very first time we walked down to the rink."

Justin stopped suddenly and because their arms were all linked, the whole line jerked to a clumsy halt. "Then maybe we walked right past our camp," he said. "What should we do?"

"So, *now* you want my opinion?" Jackie said.

"I think I see the camp," Nick said. "Can you see that light?"

"Good eyes, Nick," Jackie said. "Let's check it out."

"I sure am glad you guys can see," Justin said. Even the rims of his eyes were beginning to ache with the cold, making it hard to keep them open. "I can't make out anything."

With arms still linked, they hurried along toward the light like the characters in the *Wizard of Oz* headed for the glow of the Emerald City.

But as the structure they saw slowly took shape before them, they recognized it was much too small to be a camp. In fact, it wasn't a building at all. It was more like a small tent. Lit from within, they could see a massive silhouette moving toward what they imagined must have been the door.

Before they could turn to run, a large head seemingly without eyes or a mouth emerged that was covered with fur and frost. Then from somewhere within the furry, frosty face a deep, raspy voice thundered forth, "Who's there?"

Did the creature say more? The Adirondack kids had no idea, their six churning legs carrying them with abandon across the frigid landscape.

Chapter Six

Wandering in
a Winter Land

There was a real sense of urgency with every step taken by the Adirondack kids. Not only did they want desperately to get home – but they also hoped to avoid any more unwelcome surprises that might be lurking in the falling snow just in front of them, or behind them, or next to them, even a few feet away.

Justin didn't like what was underneath them either. He didn't care if there were twelve or more inches of ice below their feet strong enough to hold a snow-mobile or a deer or even a large hairy creature in a tent. Because he knew underneath that ice below his feet there was water as deep and dark as the evening sky. If it weren't for the warm fellowship of his friends, he imagined he would just sit down and begin to cry.

"I can't believe we saw the abdominal snowman," Nick said, as they continued on the move. He was literally shaking, and it wasn't from the cold. "Did you see how big it was?"

Jackie couldn't let it go, common sense quickly returning to her normally level head. "You mean the *abominable* snowman," she said. "Abdominal has something to do with your tummy. Abominable is like a monster. And just so you know, that was not the abominable snowman."

"Well, if it wasn't the abdominabable snowman, what was it then?" Nick said. "Big Foot?"

Jackie stopped walking. "Listen," she said, sternly and with conviction. "It wasn't a snowman, it wasn't Big Foot and it wasn't Old Man Winter."

"I know it wasn't Old Man Winter," Nick said.

"Good," Jackie said.

"I know that, because Old Man Winter is a lot nicer," Nick said, and grinned.

Jackie moved like she was about to tackle him.

Nick squealed and pulled away to avoid contact. "You said no body checks," he said.

Justin quickly interrupted to save his friend and maintain their link. "Who do you think it was, Jackie?" he said.

Calm returned to Jackie's face. "I think it was an ice fisherman," she said. "And I think if we hadn't run away like little scared rabbits, he probably could have shown us the way back home." She took a deep breath. "At least it's a sign the ice is still good and thick where we are."

"I didn't run like a scared rabbit," Nick said. "If I had run like a rabbit, it would been like this." Trying to hop he tugged their human chain forward and then tripped, causing all three of them to tumble to the ground.

Snow slid up Justin's coat sleeve and down into his boots and even into his nose. "Thanks, Nick," he said.

"I didn't do it on purpose," Nick said.

Jackie, still holding her holiday bag, gathered herself, and stood up. "We made it," she said.

Justin liked the tone of her voice. "What is it, Jackie?" he said.

"Look what Nick tripped on," Jackie said.

"Rocks!" Nick said. "It's the shoreline! We're home!"

Jackie carefully crossed over the rocks and moved onto the land. "But this can't be," she said.

Justin rose to his feet and hobbled over to join her. "What's wrong?" he said.

Jackie didn't answer him. She kept walking as if she knew exactly where she was going. Justin and Nick moved quickly to stay with her, dodging first a small woodpile and then a large rack holding several kayaks that were covered snug with tarps. When they finally caught up with Jackie, she was standing in front of a door which looked like it had been open for quite some time, snow drifting into the entranceway.

"Do you know this place?" Justin said.

"Do you know where we are?" Nick said.

"I should know, and so should you," Jackie said. "This is my family's island camp."

Chapter Seven

Safe and Snowbound

Justin had been at Jackie's summer home, Salsberry Island, plenty of times before, but with the falling snow, the growing darkness and the panic in his chest that came and went in waves, he never would have recognized it. "We were that far off?" he said, his voice quivering. "We went in the total opposite direction?" Images of his parents' worried faces flashed through his mind, and he felt his stomach churn.

"Why is the door wide open?" Nick said. "You don't think the abdominable guy beat us here, do you?" He stopped. "I said that word wrong again, didn't I?"

"Why don't you go in and check for us," Jackie said. Nick stood paralyzed as she brushed by him and checked the door handle. "The latch is fine. The wind must have blown it open." She reached behind the door and handed Nick a broom. "You sweep the snow out, and I'll start a fire. We'll get warm and make a plan."

Jackie wasted no time and soon had them all sitting around a crackling fire, which was filling the room with light and heat.

Nick wedged a chair against both the front and the back doors. "Not for the Big Foot," he said. "It's so the wind won't blow either one of them open again." Justin and Jackie didn't believe him, but they said nothing, quietly glad for the extra sense of security.

Justin was thankful to finally peel off his snow pants and jacket. He placed his wet boots and mittens on the warm hearth of the fireplace next to those of his friends. *Jackie's island camp?* He couldn't get the thought out of his head. There were many places on the lake where due to the steady flow of water from inlets the ice could be so thin it could not carry any weight at all. He knew he was never to venture out onto the lake any time of year without letting his parents know exactly where he was going and for how long. Of course, what had happened was not intentional. But neither were terrible accidents.

"Well, we're safe," Jackie said.

Justin thought Jackie was somehow reading his mind. "Yes, but our parents don't know where we are," he said.

"And it's Christmas Eve!" Nick said.

Jackie walked over to peer out a window. "Still snowing," she said. "Well, I guess there is only one thing we can do."

"Cry?" Nick said.

"I don't think that's her big idea," Justin said. Actually, he could not remember a time he had ever seen Jackie cry, except some times when Nick was

27

Jackie walked over to peer out the window.
"It's still snowing," she said.
"I guess there's only one thing we can do."

driving her crazy. But that was a different kind of crying. He looked around the dimly lit room, the walls alive with their shadows. He could not imagine what she had in mind. "So, what should we do?"

Jackie turned and raised her hands. "What else?" she said. "We get ready for Christmas!"

Chapter Eight

Use Your Imagination!

"First we have to get in the mood," Jackie said. "Let's decorate." She pulled a flashlight from a desk drawer and began hustling up the bare wood stairs to the second floor. "I'll be right back. You two look around and be thinking, 'Christmas.'"

"What's this?" Nick said. He pointed to a small box with dials that was sitting on the desk in which Jackie had found the flashlight.

Justin shrugged. "Jackie's dad saves a lot of old stuff like that," he said. "It looks like it has an antenna."

"Maybe it's a radio," Nick said. He found an on/off switch and clicked it back and forth. "Nothing," he said. "Whatever it is, it must be broken."

"It *is* a radio," Jackie said. She was already bounding back down the stairs holding three socks. "And it's not broken."

"It's too bad we don't have any electricity out here to turn it on," Justin said.

Jackie laughed. "Are you kidding? We have a back-up for almost everything," she said. "It probably just needs new batteries." She handed Justin the flash-light. "Right next to the sink in the kitchen is a junk drawer. Bring any you can find."

When Justin returned with a small plastic bag full of batteries, Jackie and Nick were setting up a small stepladder near the fireplace. "What are you hang-ing on the ceiling?" he said.

"Nothing," Jackie said. "This is going to be our tree."

Nick looked at Justin and shrugged.

"Will you two please use your imaginations?" Jackie said. "Look at it." She used her hands for emphasis. "It's shaped like a triangle. It's broader at the bottom than at the top." Pleased with her description, she asked them, "Now what do you see?"

"I see a ladder," Nick said.

Jackie rolled up a sock and threw it at him. "Go hang up your stocking," she said.

Nick walked over to the fireplace, unrolled his sock and held it up to the mantle. "Hung on the chimney with care," he said, and grinned. "In hopes that me, good old Saint Nick, soon would be there!" The sock slipped from his hand and fell directly into the flames below. The sock disappeared almost instantly. The orange flicker from the fire masked his blushing cheeks. "Sorry, Jackie. Do you have another stocking for me?"

"Yes, don't worry about it," Jackie said. "I only brought down socks that didn't have matches. But be careful, would you?"

Justin handed the bag of batteries to Jackie.

"Perfect," she said. "What are the scissors for?"

"I found them in the drawer with the batteries," Justin said. "If you have some paper, I thought I could cut out some snowflakes. We learned how to do that the last day of school before vacation."

Jackie popped open the back of the radio and snapped several of the larger batteries in place. "You can use some of the newspapers over in the kindling box," she said. "Snowflakes will be perfect ornaments to put on our tree." She turned a nob and the old radio crackled to life, but the only sound was static. "I was afraid this might happen. We're never sure what kind of a signal we'll get out here."

"Let me help," Nick said. Before Jackie could stop him, he grabbed the radio from her hands and scoped the built-in antenna out as far as it could go. Suddenly there was music, and he beamed.

"There's still a little static," Justin said. "But it's pretty clear."

"And it's Christmas music," Jackie said. "Great job, Nick. Why don't you put the radio back on the desk and I'll get something for us to eat."

"Eat?" Nick said. He had forgotten how absolutely famished he was. "You have something to eat?" He set the radio down, let go of the antenna, and the music stopped. He touched the antenna, and the music started playing again.

Justin laughed. "It looks like if we're going to have music, you'll have to hold the antenna all night," he said.

Nick frowned. "I'll only hold it until you bring the food," he said, and then remembered the frosting cookie sandwich he had stuffed into his pocket earlier. With his free hand he reached for it and moaned. "Mush," he said, licking the frosting and crumbs from his sticky fingers. He looked at Jackie. "I hope you've got something really good."

Chapter Nine

'Twas the Night Before Christmas

Justin continued to cut out paper snowflakes, while Nick held the antenna. Holiday music rang out from the old radio without interruption. No announcer. No advertisements. Just *Jingle Bells, Rudolph the Red-nosed Reindeer* and *Silent Night*. He called out to Jackie who had once again disappeared into the kitchen. "What could you even have here to eat?" he said. "You closed up your camp for the winter months ago."

Jackie reappeared and handed them each their stocking. The red and white hook from a fat peppermint candy cane stuck out of the top of each one.

Nick cheered. "I still get my Christmas Eve candy cane," he said. "I'm not putting *this* sock over the fireplace."

"I didn't even notice you took the socks away," Justin said, as he probed the inside of his stocking. He pulled out a piece of chocolate that was shaped like a hockey stick, and a chocolate snowman wrapped in colorful foil that glittered in the firelight. "Thanks, Jackie." Then he noticed her holiday shopping bag was missing. "You didn't give us the presents you bought for your parents, did you?"

Jackie shook her head. "No, I bought these things for both of you," she said. "Why do you think I wanted you to wait outside in Inlet while I was in the store?"

"You're sneaky," Nick said, struggling to rip the clear cellophane from his candy cane with his teeth and still hold the radio antenna to keep the music playing.

"I was going to give the chocolate hockey sticks to you at our celebration party after we win our game," Jackie said. "This just seemed like the right time, instead."

"It's the perfect time," Justin said. Then he handed her a small fistful of paper snowflakes – all the same shape, but all different sizes.

"You hold onto them," Jackie said. She found some Scotch tape in the desk drawer and walked over to the stepladder. "Bring them here and help me decorate our tree."

Justin joined her as one by one Jackie removed from his hands the paper snowflakes, taping them up and down the length of each leg of the ladder. "Seriously," he said. "Do you think every snowflake is different?"

Jackie shrugged. "I like to think so," she said. "But I really don't know how anyone could say for sure." She stepped back to examine their imaginary tree. "Finished," she said. "And we still have more

35

flakes. Let's tape some on the windows."

"I'm getting kind of bored here," Nick said. He was still standing next to the desk with a hand touching the radio antenna. "Can we do something together now?"

Justin handed Jackie his last snowflake. "Like what?" he said.

"Every year my mom reads *'Twas the Night Before Christmas* to us out loud," Nick said. "Why don't we do that?"

"We'd better think of something else to do," Justin said.

Nick frowned. "Why?" he said.

"Well," Justin said. "Do you see your mom here right now?" He was more than slightly irritated with the reminder that none of them were at home with their parents, who surely by now were worried sick about them. "So unless someone starts reading that story on the radio, we'll have to think of something else to do." He paused. "Unless you have it memorized."

Nick's frown turned to sadness. "It was just an idea," he said. "And it's not a story. It's a poem."

Justin realized he had hurt his friend and that bothered him almost as badly as the worry over their dilemma. "I'm sorry," he said.

"Maybe Nick's idea will work," Jackie said.

Nick perked up. "It will?" he said.

"Forget about the radio," Jackie said. She set another log on the fire. "Let's all sit on the couch in front of the fireplace."

Nick hesitated, but then did let go of the antenna. "Hey, the music is still playing," he said, and slightly turned down the sound. Then he hurried to join his friends, making a giant leap onto the couch next to Jackie, who was seated in the middle.

"Okay," Justin said. "How is Nick's idea going to work?"

"Well, think about it," Jackie said. "How many times have we all heard that poem?"

"Like a million," Nick said.

Justin protested. "Maybe you've heard it a lot before, but not me," he said.

"But we've all heard it," Jackie said. "So, why don't we put our memories all together and see how much of it we can recite?"

Justin shrugged. "I guess we can try," he said.

Nick was thrilled. "I vote I start," he said.

"Okay, Nick," Jackie said. "You begin."

With holiday music still streaming from the radio, Nick smiled and looked at the fire. The light appeared to make his eyes sparkle, and that made Justin smile.

"'Twas the night before Christmas and all through the house," Nick began. "Not a creature was stirring, not even a mouse."

"Okay, my turn," Jackie said. "The stockings were hung by the chimney with care – "

Nick interrupted. "In hopes that Saint Nicholas soon would be there," he said. "I just had to say the part with my name in it." He grinned, and looked at

37

Justin. "It's your turn."

Justin wasn't at all sure what came next. "I think I know it," he said. "The children were nestled all snug in their beds –" He paused. "Oh yeah – while visions of sugarplums danced in their heads."

"That's right," Jackie said.

"Now Dasher! Now Dancer! Now Prancer and Vixen!" Nick said. "On Comet! On Cupid! On Donner and Blitzen!"

"That's not the next line," Jackie said.

"But that's all I can remember without some clues," Nick said. "Help me, Justin."

Justin shrugged. "How would I know?" he said. "You're the one who has heard it a million times."

"I know what the right line is," Jackie said. "And mama in her 'kerchief, and I in my cap, had just settled our brains for a long winter's –"

"Settled our brains?" Justin said. "There's some weird lines in there." He leaned forward to look past Jackie at Nick. "No wonder you like this poem so much."

"That's the clue I needed," Nick said. "I know the line after that one." He cleared his throat to make a dramatic delivery. "When out on the lawn there arose such a clatter –"

"Shhh!" Jackie said. "Did you hear that noise outside?"

"Yes," Justin said. "It sounded like snowmobiles, but it stopped."

Nick was annoyed. "Let me finish," he said.

"When out on the lawn there arose such a clatter, I sprang from my bed –"

Bang-Bang-Bang!

The knocking on the front door was so fierce it seemed to make the whole camp shake.

It also shook Nick, who barely completed his line. "To see what was the matter."

Chapter Ten

Reunion

Bang-Bang-Bang!

"Do you think it's the Big Foot?" Nick said. He raised his feet into the seat of the couch and tried to make his body disappear by using his knees to press himself back into the cushions.

"Stop it," Jackie said. "There are several possibilities of who it could be." But she didn't name one.

Nick whispered. "It's hard to tell over the radio, but I think there's more than one person out there," he said.

Not one of the Adirondack kids budged. In fact, by the third round of banging on the door, it was hard to tell they were breathing.

There was a single loud and violent ***thud*** against the door.

"They're trying to break in," Justin said.

Jackie was quiet, and as paralyzed as the boys.

There was a second dull thud and the chair that was wedged against the door began to move.

Nick drew in his breath and closed his eyes. Then he squeaked like a mouse. "We're doomed," he said.

By the third thud, the chair dislodged and slid across the room, crashing to the floor. Several bodies covered with snow and faces covered with hoods, masks and goggles barged into the camp.

That was when the Adirondack kids let out a collective scream.

"Jackie?" one of masked men called.

"Justin?" called another. "Are you here?"

Boots stomped as hats and facemasks were removed, and terror transformed into relief for everyone in the room.

"Mom! Dad!" Jackie said. She launched from the couch and across the room into their arms.

Then there were six happy adults in the room on their knees, holding three very happy children.

"We were so worried about you," Mrs. Robert said as Justin's head buried into her shoulder.

"We didn't get lost on purpose," Nick said to his mother and father.

"We know," said Mr. Barnes. "We're just so very thankful all of you are all right."

"How did you know we were here?" Justin said. Then he noticed a seventh hulking figure standing in the doorway. Snow, like confetti, was swirling all around him.

Nick actually saw him first. "It's the Abominable Snowman!" he said. Then, "Hey, did you hear me? I said it right that time!"

The large man stepped into the room and shut the door to keep the cold and relentlessly blowing snow outside. "Are you talking about me?" the man said, his voice booming. "I'm no snowman." He flipped back his hood and removed his large wool cap.

"Captain McBride!" Jackie said.

"We all have the dear captain to thank for helping us find you," Mrs. Robert said.

The captain took a long step forward and quickly surveyed the room. There was the holiday music playing – the fire raging – the custom tree with its paper snowflakes. He nodded. "Very resourceful," he said. Then he looked at Jackie. "Not surprising, knowing you."

"We thought you stored your mail boat and went south for the winter," Justin said.

"Not this year," the captain said. "Not ever again."

"He's fallen in love with ice fishing," Mr. Robert said. "And how fortunate for us all that he did."

"What do you say we put that fire out, and get everyone back home now," Jackie's father said. "While it's still Christmas Eve!"

Chapter Eleven

The Abominable Snowcat

Justin continued rolling and packing and molding snow at the edge of the skating rink. It was Christmas at camp after all! The night before seemed like a dream – some of it a good dream, and some of it really bad. He stood back to admire his work of art.

"So this is what you've been working on all afternoon?" It was Jackie, and she was holding an old broom. "Now I see why you wanted some bristles."

"I've been working on it almost *all day*," Justin said, and dropped to his knees to finish carving a groove that better defined the legs and feet of his creation. "I can't wait until Nick sees it." He looked up at the head towering just above him. "I hope he remembers to bring the eyes."

Jackie smiled. "So, did you get any presents this morning that you didn't expect?" she said.

Justin stopped working. "Do you mean the hockey jersey?" he said. "It was fantastic! I didn't expect that at all. You had this planned a long time ago, didn't you?"

Jackie smiled. "I knew you would join me for the

"So this is what you've been working
on all afternoon?" Jackie said.

challenge," she said. "I thought it would be nice if we had something to make us look like a team. But Mom and Dad even surprised me by ordering jerseys for all of us."

"Yahoo!" It was Nick, lifting his legs high as he sprinted toward them from his camp next door. The sound of the snow crunching under his feet as he got closer reminded Justin of the same sound his dad made at breakfast when he chomped on cornflakes.

"Hey guys," Nick said, with arms waving and scarf flying. "Look at what I just opened." Out of breath, he stopped in front of them and dropped to his knees. "What do you think?" He stretched his arms wide to show off his brand new hockey jersey. It was as white as new fallen snow, with bright blue trim. And on the chest in bold block letters – **INLET** – which were also in blue with red trim.

"It looks great, Nick," Justin said.

"I like this part the best," Nick said, and turned his shoulders enough to reveal his upper back. There was his last name, printed in smaller blue block letters – **BARNES**.

Jackie nodded in agreement with Justin, but with hands on her hips. "Yes, it does look great, Nick," she said. "There's only one problem."

"What?" Nick said. "My name isn't spelled wrong, is it?"

"Don't look up at me with those big sad eyes," Jackie said. She pointed her finger at him. "You're not supposed to wear that jersey until the game tomorrow."

Nick looked relieved. "You scared me," he said, "I thought I did something really bad."

Jackie scooped some snow to throw at Nick, but Justin intervened. "Hey, bring that snow over here," he said. "I think I can use it." He stood and walked all the way around his handiwork. "Okay, Nick," he said. "Did you bring something green for the eyes?"

Nick reached into the pocket of his snow pants. "Right here," he said, and handed Justin two green lollipops.

"Perfect," Justin said, and stretched high to position the round pops into the eye sockets. He punched each one stick first into its hollowed-out area, and used Jackie's snow to fill in each cavity. "The eyes have to be just the right shape." Then he pulled a piece of charred coal from his own pocket and pressed it into place for the nose.

Jackie snapped several bristles from the old broom. "I know where these go," she said, and poked half a dozen into each cheek.

"Now it's done except for the mouth," Justin said. "I've got some solid red candy canes I'm going to snap apart and use for that." He looked at Nick. "So, do you still think a snowman would have been better?"

"I do like it," Nick said. "It kind of reminds me of the Great Spinks of Egypt."

"That would be the Sphinx of Egypt," Jackie said. "Not Spinks."

Nick shrugged. "But you knew what I meant," he said.

"You did a great job, Justin," Jackie said. "It looks just like Dax."

"Except a whole lot bigger," Nick said. "Hey, I have an idea."

"Uh-oh," Jackie said.

"No, really, I do," Nick said.

Jackie sighed. "Okay. What is it?" she said.

"Well, our team is called, INLET, right?" Nick said.

Jackie nodded. "My mom had a relative who played on the first team that ever played ice hockey in Inlet almost a hundred years ago," she said. "She still has old pictures of him in his uniform and that's where she and my dad got the inspiration for our team name and our jerseys."

"So, what's your idea, Nick?" Justin said.

"I vote we should be the INLET something," Nick said. "You know, have a mascot."

"That's a good idea," Justin said. "What do you think, Jackie?"

"Well, maybe," Jackie said.

"Great," Nick said. "I vote we are the INLET LOONIES."

"You've got to be kidding," Jackie said.

"What's wrong with that name?" Nick said. "Loons are right here on our lake."

"I know," Jackie said. "I'm standing right here next to one!" She turned to Justin. "This isn't going to work. It will take us forever to agree on a name."

"What about this?" Justin said. He pointed to the snow sculpture before them.

47

"The INLET SNOWMEN?" Nick said.

"No," Jackie said. "I get it. The INLET SNOW-CATS. Right, Justin?"

"Exactly," Justin said. "And Dax can be our real live mascot."

"And this statue can be the giant symbol right here at our official home arena," Jackie said. "I love it."

Nick laughed. "I'll bet Old Forge doesn't even have a whole name," he said.

Jackie winced. "I'm afraid they do," she said.

"Afraid?" Nick said.

Justin turned to her. "What is their name, Jackie?"

"The Hammers," Jackie said.

"They're called the *Hammers*?" Justin said. "The Old Forge *Hammers*?"

Jackie nodded.

Nick's smile disappeared. "I knew it," he said. "We are definitely doomed."

Chapter Twelve

Hammer Time

Justin had shoveled the entire hockey rink clean from snow all by himself. Even after working on his sculpture of Dax nearly all of Christmas day, it had still been hard to fall asleep. After breakfast this morning he needed something to do to keep his nervous mind occupied. He could not believe how different camp and the boathouse and the whole landscape looked coated with winter. Patches of the ice reflected the clear blue sky, and the crisp, cold morning air made the inside of his nose sting. Now seated on the dock and lacing up his rented skates, he could see Nick dressed in his helmet and jersey, making his way along the rocky shoreline to join him. This was it. For weeks Jackie had been waiting for this day – a day he wished was still weeks away!

"You have the rink ready?" Nick said. He dropped his stick and skates on the dock and sat down next to his friend. "I wanted to come over early to help you."

"I didn't mind doing it at all," Justin said, as he punched a foot into his second skate. "What time was it when you left your camp?"

"It was around 11:30," Nick said.

"It's that late already?" Justin said. "I thought maybe we could use some extra time to practice." He looked at Nick's skates. "Did you rent those, too?"

Nick shook his head. "No," he said. "They didn't have any skates left in my size, so my mom found this pair for me at camp in the back of a closet." He held them up. "Someone cut the front of the blades off on both of them." He shrugged. "They're kind of ruined, but at least they fit me and look – the color matches our jerseys."

Justin slipped on his helmet and mittens, picked up his own stick and dropped from the dock into the snow. Carefully stepping onto the ice, he took a deep breath and pushed off with his left skate causing him to glide slowly forward.

"That's no fair," Nick said. "You can already skate really good."

Justin hardly heard him. He was concentrating on his balance and getting a feel for the skates. He remembered the hard shell of his rollerblades encasing his leg from the calf down. They made his ankles feel almost locked in place and secure. His ankles in these ice skates? Not so much. Pushing off with his right foot, he dared to pick up a little speed.

"Not bad for a rookie!" It was Jackie. With a bag in one hand and skates tied and dangling from the end of the hockey stick she was carrying over her shoulder, she hurried onto the dock and sat down next to Nick.

Justin turned to wave and lost his balance. Falling on his side, he slid until being stopped by the foot-high board that served as the rink's border. Returning to his feet was not all that easy. Trying without success to use his stick like a cane, he fought first to his knees, then to his feet. "I wish we had more time to practice," he said.

"You'll do fine," Jackie said. While Nick was still struggling to lace his second skate, Jackie had both of her skates on, and was out on the ice. She pulled a puck from her pocket and tossed it out in front of her. She captured the black disc quickly with the blade of her stick and like a flash was down the length of the rink and back again. After another full loop, she stopped where Justin remained standing. "Come on, Justin, get loosened up." And she was off again.

Justin admired her spirit and wondered how she could feel so good about the game, when he and Nick were obviously so inexperienced and unprepared. But her confidence was contagious and gave him the courage to try. He did fall down again, and again, but kept getting back up and soon he was moving forward and even turning with greater assurance and speed.

"Attack the goal with me, Justin," Jackie said, and the two of them began skating side by side. "Keep your stick down on the ice."

Easily controlling the puck, Jackie veered off to the left, creating separation from her teammate. She flicked the puck forward to him as he approached the goal and it ricocheted off the blade of his stick, barely missing the slot for the score. Instead, it banged off the front of the box.

Justin was so excited that he forgot to turn and went headlong over the board and into a bank of snow.

"That's okay, Justin," Jackie said. "Great try."

"Yes, that was awesome, Justin," said someone from the shoreline.

Justin, Jackie and Nick all turned to see four hockey players standing side by side wearing black facemasks and dressed in full black uniforms accented with gold stripes and letters. They were clapping their black gloves together very slowly and in perfect unison. With the exception of height, they appeared identical.

The Hammers had arrived.

Chapter Thirteen

Rules are Rules

It did not take long for the Hammers to lace up their skates. Leaving their large black sports bags on the Barnes' family dock, which they used as their bench, all four members of the visiting team were on the ice quickly, passing and shooting with speed and precision.

Justin, Jackie and Nick patiently waited on the Robert's family dock while the visitors had their turn to warm up for the contest.

"They're weaving around so fast, they're making me dizzy," Nick said.

Justin couldn't take his eyes off them. "Who are they, Jackie?"

"I know Braedon the best," she said. "He's the one you met in Inlet and he's the one who challenged us."

Nick corrected her. "You mean he challenged *you*," he said. "And I remember which one he is just by looking at the size of his neck!"

"What about the other three, Jackie," Justin said. "Do you even know them?"

Jackie shook her head. "Not very well," she said.

"They were on the class trip when I met them." She pointed. "The one who is skating really fast? That's Corey."

"What about the one who has the bottom of his facemask pulled down under his chin?" Justin said.

"The one who is breathing really hard?" Jackie said. "That's Drake."

"And the short one?" Nick said. "He hasn't stopped skating for a single second since getting out there."

"I think his name is Keegan," Jackie said.

"Where is *our* fourth player?" asked Justin.

Before she could answer, Braedon called from the center of the rink. "Miss Jackie Salsberry," he said. "Are you ready to go over the rules?"

"Okay, this is it," Jackie said to her teammates. "Come on, and I'll introduce you." She and Justin helped Nick off the dock. As soon as they stepped onto the ice Nick's ankles began to wobble.

Nick whispered. "Please don't let go of me, you guys," he said.

With Justin holding one arm and Jackie holding the other, they assisted Nick across the ice and joined their four opponents at the center of the rink for formal introductions and to review the rules.

Nick noticed that the short player kept staring at him.

"Nice white skates," Keegan said, the sound of his voice muffled by his facemask. "Are they your mom's or your sister's?"

"I don't have a sister," Nick said. He looked down at

his feet and then at Jackie. "Are these skates for girls?"

Jackie shrugged. "It's no big deal," she said. "Boys wear figure skates, too."

"Yeah," Keegan said. "Black ones."

"So, no one ruined the front of these blades?" Nick said.

"Figure skates are made that way," Jackie said. "The jagged part is called a toe pick."

Nick moaned and Keegan laughed. "Are your ankles shaking because you're nervous, or because you've never been on skates before?" he said.

Braedon pulled the bottom of his own nylon face-mask down. "That's enough, Keegan," he said, making it clear who was in charge of the team.

Keegan didn't stop. "We're the Old Forge Hammers," he said.

"We know who you are," Jackie said.

"We're the Inlet Snowcats," Justin said.

"The Snowcats or The Scaredy Cats?" Keegan said.

Braedon turned to Keegan and stared him down.

"All right, all right," Keegan said. "I'll be quiet." He skated away. And Drake, the heavy breather, joined him.

"Okay, Miss Jackie Sals –" Braedon began.

Jackie interrupted him. "My name is just Jackie," she said. "Not Miss Jackie Salsberry. It's just, Jackie."

Braedon raised his eyebrows. "Okay," he said.

Before the Hammer leader could say more, Jackie continued. "And here are the pond hockey rules," she said. "We play two 15-minute halves with a 2-

55

minute intermission. All goals have to be scored on the attackers' side of the ice and no one can camp out in front of the goal. There is no touching the puck with your stick above your waist and no passes above the knees. If you touch the puck with your stick above your waist or pass above your knees, the other team gets the puck. There are no slap shots and no body checking. If there is a slap shot or a body check, it is a penalty and the player is ejected from the game. The penalty shot will be taken from the center of the rink. Agreed?"

Braedon smiled. "Agreed," he said.

Justin hardly understood anything Jackie had said, but as always was impressed with her knowledge and boldness.

Nick whispered to Justin. "What does *ejected* mean?"

"I'm not sure," Justin said. "I think it means if you hit the puck too hard or slam into somebody, you're kicked out of the game for good."

Nick nodded and smiled. He liked that idea.

Jackie's glare never left Braedon. "Anything else?" she said.

"Yes," Braedon said. "We agreed to start at noon and I see you only have three players."

Jackie didn't flinch. "We have a fourth player coming," she said.

Braedon smiled again. But it wasn't like a friendly smile. "Well, I don't know when you expect your fourth man to get here, but according to my watch it is 10 minutes to noon right now, and we will begin right at noon," he said. "We'll play three against three until your fourth man gets here." He never stopped smiling. "Agreed?"

Justin noticed Jackie glance toward the shoreline, as if looking for her friend. For the first time since talking about the pond hockey challenge he thought she looked nervous. But her voice never wavered.

"Agreed," Jackie said.

The fourth Hammer, who had been as silent as Keegan had been loud, finally spoke up. The one named, Corey. "Where's the clock?" he said.

Braedon looked at Jackie. "You are the home team," he said. "Where's your time clock?"

Justin could tell Jackie had forgotten all about a clock and came to her rescue. "I left it in my room up at camp," he said. "It will only take me a minute to get it." He let go of Nick's arm, causing his friend to lose his balance and fall backwards. Jackie still had Nick's other arm, but the sudden jolt took her by surprise, causing her to crash to the ice with him.

Keegan simply shook his head and chuckled as he and Drake skated past them to their bench.

"Noon sharp … Jackie," Braedon said, as he and Corey took off to join their friends.

Chapter Fourteen

Let the Game Begin!

"Why did you bring Dax with you?" Nick said. He and Jackie were waiting next to the towering snow sculpture that so resembled their team's real-life mascot.

Justin had the wind-up alarm clock in his hand and turned to see his loyal calico had, indeed, slipped through the door behind him. She had jumped from skate print to skate print to follow him all the way down to the rink. He sighed. "I'll take her back up to camp," he said.

Braedon called from center ice. He was tapping his fat-fingered hockey glove onto the watch on his wrist. "It's 5 minutes past noon," he said. "You're already breaking the rules."

Jackie seized the clock from Justin. "There's not enough time to take Dax back up the hill," she said. She set the timer for 15 minutes and balanced the clock on top of the snow sculpture's head. "We're not going to give them any excuses for when they lose. We have to start playing right now." She marched toward the rink. "Let's go."

Dax sat looking up toward the face of the giant snow sculpture.

"That's you, Dax," Justin said. He took off his mitten and bent down to pet her, burying his fingers into her warm fur. "You stay right here now. It's your job to cheer us on."

Jackie, Nick and Justin stepped back onto the ice, and in that order.

"Corey will wait over by that snow cat thing you made and start the clock," Braedon said. "We'll take turns with who sits out until your fourth man gets here."

"Unless he's too afraid to show up," Keegan said.

Jackie ignored the comment. "Without a referee, how should we handle dropping the puck?" she said.

"It'll be easy," Braedon said. He passed her the puck. "You guys can have it first."

"Okay," Jackie said. "Then after a team scores, the other team gets a turn."

"Fine with us," Braedon said. He called out to Corey. "Go ahead, start the clock."

Jackie took off like a shot. Not even Keegan could catch her, and within seconds, the Snowcats had their first goal.

"Way to go, Jackie!" Justin said. He had hardly moved, and Nick definitely had not moved. In fact, it looked like Nick was going to be standing in the same place with his ankles bent inward and nearly touching the ice for the duration of the contest.

The Hammers answered Jackie's quick strike

immediately. With Braedon in the center, and Drake and Keegan on the wings, the three raced toward the Snowcats' goal.

Jackie challenged Braedon, who had the puck. Keegan easily skated by Justin, received a pass from his team leader, and scored.

Keegan laughed. "Score's all tied up," he said.

Jackie called out to Nick. "We need you down here by our goal to help with defense," she said.

Nick dropped to his knees and began crawling across the ice. "I'm coming," he said.

It was the Snowcats' turn again. While Nick was still crawling to get into defensive position, Jackie was already on the attack. "Come on, Justin." As she slowed up in an effort to allow her teammate to catch up with her, Braedon poked at her stick and freed the puck.

Keegan snatched it in an instant and was on his way toward the Snowcats' goal. There was no way Justin could change direction quick enough. Keegan was by him in a flash, swerved around Nick who was still moving on all fours, and scored. He looped back toward center ice with his arms raised. "2-1," he said.

"Substitution," Braedon said. "Corey, come in for Keegan."

Keegan frowned. "Already?" he said. He skated toward shore and removed his helmet and facemask, revealing a full head of flame red hair. "Hurry up, the time is going fast and I want to score some more."

Justin didn't think the time was going by fast enough. He tried to help Jackie, but had to concentrate more on keeping his balance than keeping the puck in play. Three times Corey swooped in to steal the puck from him, hushed as a bird of prey with wings cutting silently through the air. With each unexpected strike, the puck was suddenly gone and ushered into their goal.

Since it was against the rules for a defender to stand or lay in front of the goal, poor wobbly Nick had to stand slightly off to the side. One time he did get his stick on the puck, but knocked it directly to Drake, who thanked him as he huffed and puffed by him and scored.

The four Hammers continued to rotate in and out of the game, taking turns adding to their lead.

Braedon was the last one to punch the puck into the Snowcats' goal just before the clock's alarm mercifully sounded from the shoreline.

"Halftime!" announced Keegan. He turned off the alarm and headed toward the Hammer bench.

"Two minutes, Jackie," Braedon said.

Justin and Nick joined Jackie at the snow sculpture, where she reset the clock for the short intermission and placed it at their feet.

Nick threw his stick and plopped backwards into the snow, raising his legs into the air. "My ankles are so sore," he said. "I bet I won't be able to walk for a week."

"I'm sorry I didn't do more, Jackie," Justin said.

His head was sweating so he took off his helmet and replaced it with his bucket hat that was hanging on top of an extra hockey stick that was stuck upright in the snow. "I think I can do better."

"Better?" Nick said. "We're already behind almost ten goals. Jackie scored our only one." He sat up and reached down with both hands in an attempt to rub the outside of his skates in the area of his throbbing ankles. "I'm sorry, too. But I told you I couldn't skate."

Jackie removed her helmet as well. "I'm the one who is sorry," she said. "I really thought this was going to be fun for all of us." She paused. "But you know what?"

Justin shook his head. "What?" he said.

Nick also looked up at her.

"I don't care what happens the rest of the game," Jackie said. And then she smiled. "Because I have the two best friends in the whole world." She paused again. "And do you know what else?"

"What?" Nick said. Both he and Justin were smiling with her now.

Jackie whispered. "I have a plan."

Chapter Fifteen

Checked Out

The 2-minute alarm sounded and the Snowcats broke from their secret huddle.

Justin picked up the clock to turn it off, and wondered where Dax had gone. Her footprints appeared to circle the snow sculpture dozens of times, but then completely disappeared.

Jackie started for the rink. "Let's go, Justin," she said.

The Hammers had decided Keegan would be their team's first substitute and he was making his way toward them at the sideline.

"I'm looking for Dax," Justin said. He held up the clock. "I think the alarm scared her off."

Nick was walking gingerly next to Jackie, trying desperately to stay on his feet. He turned back to Justin and pointed. "Look up," he said.

Justin looked up and there she was, perched on the head of the snow sculpture. He laughed. "Get down here, Daxy," he said.

"Yeah," Keegan said, who was off the ice now and

marching toward them. "Come on down from there, kitty."

Justin frowned and handed the clock to Keegan. "I'll take care of my cat," he said. "You can reset the timer." Then he reached out, and without hesitation, Dax leapt into his outstretched arms. "Just one more half," he told her, as he gently set her down.

While Justin strapped his helmet back on to rejoin the action, Keegan called out to his teammates. "I don't like this at all," he said, and set the alarm for the final 15 minutes. "Nobody ever told me I was going to have to sit out half of the game."

Braedon ignored his whining teammate and looked at Jackie. "Are you ready?" he said.

Jackie nodded. "Are you?" she said.

"Totally ready," Braedon said. He looked around. "Still no fourth player?"

"Too scared, I guess," Jackie said, her face sporting a sarcastic smile.

Braedon turned to Drake. "How many goals are we ahead now?" he said. "I lost count."

Drake shrugged and looked at Corey.

Before Corey could answer, Jackie replied. "Nine," she said. "The current score is 10 to 1."

Braedon smiled. "Since we are so far ahead, we'll let you have the puck first again," he said.

"Why, thank you so much," Jackie said.

"You're welcome," Braedon said. "And don't even think about skating by us. This time we are ready for you."

Keegan yelled from his post. "Can I start the clock now?" he said.

"Yes!" Braedon said. "Now!"

At that very moment, Nick cried out and flopped to the ground.

"He made the ice crack!" Justin said, and quickly backed away.

The startled Hammers froze.

While their eyes were busy scanning the ice beneath their skates for signs of danger, Jackie was off with the puck. She was even able to take her time. With a gentle flick of her wrist, the disc entered the goal for a totally uncontested score.

"10 to 2," Jackie said, as she returned and skated past the stunned opposition. Reaching the Snowcats' side of the ice, she spun and faced them. "Your turn."

The Hammers wore black and gold, but the faces underneath their masks were turning the color of Keegan's hair.

Braedon glared at Jackie. He pulled the bottom of his black mask over his mouth again so only his penetrating eyes remained uncovered. "Go get the puck, Drake," he said.

Drake was still looking down at his feet.

"The ice is not cracking up," Braedon said, and slapped the blade of his stick on the frozen surface. "Stop worrying and get the puck."

Drake retrieved the puck and began the new attack, firing it forward to Corey, who was positioning himself on a wing. The speedster then made a short saucer pass to Braedon in the middle. A huffing-and-puffing Drake finally caught up, and once again the three formed an intimidating triangle with Braedon at the point.

Still sitting on the ice, Nick rolled out of the way, making it three Hammers against two Snowcats.

Jackie challenged Braedon and tried to steal the puck. She managed to deflect it, but Corey was there on the wing to track it down. He smacked it bouncing in the direction of the Snowcats' goal.

The daring defensive move had cost Jackie her balance and she went sprawling toward Nick who was still lying at the center of the rink.

Now it was three Hammers against one Snowcat.

The puck had stopped bouncing and was rolling toward Justin like a tiny black wheel, and Braedon was chasing it down.

But suddenly also on the chase was Dax!

Now facing the action from a seated position, Nick called out. "She thinks it's a toy," he said.

"Dax!" Justin cried. He took some short, quick steps and glided forward. "Get off the ice!"

Braedon and Dax had one focus. The puck.

Justin had one focus. Braedon.

Dax had the shortest distance to cover and reached the puck first, knocking it down with her paws and sliding with her captured prey across the width of the rink.

Then Justin met a very surprised Braedon head-on, knocking him sideways and into Drake.

All three fallen players together slid and spun across the ice, coming to rest against the boards – a squirming pile of arms and legs and skates and sticks.

For a moment there was stone cold silence.

Then a voice called out from the shore. "Body check!" It was Keegan. "That was a body check!" he said.

Jackie skated toward the twisted heap of bodies that was struggling to become disentangled.

Justin was at the top of the mound and the first one to get loose and rise up. "Where's Dax?" he said.

"She's fine," Jackie said. Together they skated to scoop her up.

Braedon finally freed himself from Drake. He righted his helmet and adjusted his gloves. "I'll be taking the penalty shot," he said.

While Justin slowly carried Dax back to the snow sculpture, he could hear behind him the *bang* of the puck against the back of the wood goal. The sound echoed across the frozen lake.

"11 to 2," Keegan said, greeting Justin on the shore. "Guess you *checked* your way out of the game." He pointed to the clock. "And it looks like we're just 10 minutes away from a Hammer win."

Holland passed the puck through Keegan's legs
and picked it up again for yet another score.

Chapter Sixteen

A Miracle on Ice

"Power play!" Keegan said, as he hurried onto the ice to substitute for Drake.

"We should let Justin play," Corey said. "He was just protecting his cat." It was the most words at one time the quiet Hammer had spoken all day.

Braedon shrugged. "Rules are rules," he said. "Right, Jackie?"

Jackie's eyes narrowed. "Rules are rules," she said. "Nick and I get the puck. Let's play."

Braedon looked at Drake. "You're out and Keegan is in," he said. "Get moving."

Drake motioned with his stick toward the sideline. "Someone's coming," he said.

Braedon turned to Jackie. "Well, it looks like your new man decided to show up after all," he said.

"It doesn't matter," Keegan said. "It's still a power play. That just makes it four of us against the three of them for the rest of the game."

"Holland!" Jackie said. "Come on, there's still time."

"Your friend's name is Holland?" Nick said. "Now that *is* a country … right?"

"There's no time for newcomers to warm up," Braedon said.

"There's no need to warm up," Jackie said. She dropped the puck on the ice and slapped it back to the new Snowcat who had just stepped into the rink, skates laced up and ready to go.

"Hey," Nick said. "You're going the wrong way."

Jackie ignored him and took off for the Hammer goal, drawing Drake with her.

Holland filled the spot left open by Drake and barely entering the Hammers' territory, unleashed a shot. Like an arrow hitting a perfect bulls-eye – **Bang** – the puck found its mark.

"That was … great," Nick said.

Justin cheered. "11 to 3," he said.

Braedon looked at the goal and then back at Holland, who had already retreated into defensive position.

"Lucky shot," Keegan said, who noticed the large block letters on the back of the newcomer's jersey. "**MIRACLE**?" he said. "That's your last name?"

Facing them with knees bent and stick on the ice, the new Snowcat simply nodded.

Keegan looked at Jackie and laughed. "Well, you're going to need a miracle to win this game," he said.

"Just play," Jackie said as she skated by.

This time the Hammers advanced, skating in single file, and then fanned out across the width of the rink. They zipped by Nick, who had become a fixture at the rink's middle, with Braedon controlling the puck.

Drake moved in behind Braedon. Holland slowly skated backward, waiting patiently for the lead Hammer to make his move.

As Braedon dropped the puck and swerved away to leave it for his trailing teammate, Holland swooped in, swiped it, and took another shot just over center ice.

Bang.

"11 to 4," Justin called.

"We know the score," Keegan said, clearly irritated.

In an attempt to compete with Holland during the Hammers' next possession, Braedon also tried taking a long shot from just over center ice. He wasn't even close and Holland easily tracked the puck down while Jackie again took off for the Hammers' goal.

With stick ready in the passing lane, Jackie received a perfect strike, the entire length of the rink, from her teammate. A visibly rattled visiting team was scored on again.

Justin continued to call out the tally. "11 to 5," he said.

After every unanswered Snowcat goal, the Hammers regrouped, plotted, failed to score and regrouped again.

After chuckling with one another in the first half, it was all arguing among the black and gold the second half.

Keegan grew as quiet as Corey when, on another play, Holland passed the puck through his legs and picked it up again for yet another score.

Drake had long ago removed his mask and was gasping for air in the futile attempt to keep pace up and down the rink with the Jackie-Holland duo. In fact, his rapid breath was producing so many puffs of cloudy vapor, his head looked like it had vanished in the fog.

With Dax at his side and the clock ticking away, Justin cheerfully called out the scores. "11 to 6. 11 to 7. 11 to 8. 11 to 9." And then. "11 to 10."

"How much time is left?" Keegan said.

Justin looked up at the clock sitting on the sculpture's head. "Less than a minute," he said.

It was one last huddle for the Hammers. As the team split apart it was immediately clear to Jackie and Holland what their opponents had planned. Each Hammer would occupy a corner at their own end of the rink and would play keep-away with the puck until the alarm rang out indicating their victory.

Braedon called out to Justin. "You have to tell us when it is down to the last few seconds," he said.

There was no Snowcat huddle.

Nick held his position in the center of the rink, while Jackie and Holland immediately took off after the puck, hoping for an interception.

The Hammers had not been able to score since Holland entered the game, but were masterful at their stall, passing the puck to each other from side to side and corner to corner.

The sound of Snowcats' blades sliced through the

72

air as they carved up the ice in chase. Despite their superior skating skills, not a single Snowcat stick came even close to touching the puck.

Braedon called out to Justin again. "How much time is left?" he said.

Justin's worried voice replied. "15 seconds!" he said.

Braedon looked at Corey, who controlled the puck in the right corner near the goal. Jackie knew it was now or never and skated straight at him.

"Now!" the Hammer leader commanded, and Corey slapped the puck in an effort to send it deep into Snowcat territory, making it impossible for Jackie or Holland to return with it in time for a score.

As the puck glided past Jackie, for its intended journey down the length of the rink, Holland dove forward and was just able to nick it with a stick, causing it to slightly change direction.

"Stop the puck, Nick!" Jackie cried.

Nick's eyes widened as he realized he was the Snowcats' final hope. He stiffened his ankles and forced himself up onto his toe-picks. Managing two quick tip-toes toward the puck before tripping and falling face first onto the ice, his own stick flew from his hand and slid sideways intercepting the fast-moving puck and stopping it cold.

It was the break the home team had been waiting for.

"10 seconds!" an excited Justin reported.

Holland was on the puck in a flash and easily brushed by Braedon and Drake, who were attempting to close in on the Snowcat from their corners at center ice. Corey was blocked in his corner by Jackie, which left only Keegan to stop the "Miracle Worker."

Holland's stick pulled back for a shot and Keegan raced forward at full speed in an attempt to block it.

"5 seconds," Justin called. "4 – 3 ..."

It was a fake shot, and by the time Keegan realized Holland had no intention of firing, he was moving with such tremendous force he flew by and over the sideboards. In vain, he tried to maintain his balance. Stumbling forward onto shore he finally came to rest with his black helmet planted into the chest of the giant white sculpture.

With the only pesky defender out of way, and Justin calling out the final two seconds, Holland delivered the puck.

"2," Justin said. Then, *bang*, as the puck reached the back of the Hammer goal in unison with the scorekeeper's, "1."

Keegan had pulled his head from his stuck helmet and was seated between the Snowcat's feet just in time to hear the bang of the puck, followed by another sound from directly above him. His impact had loosened the sculpture's head. As it broke off and descended, it carried the screaming clock along with it. A small pile of snow, whiskers and coal landed directly in his lap.

74

"11 to 11!" Justin said. "It's a tie!" He looked at Keegan and smiled. "You can turn the alarm off now."

Chapter Seventeen

Sweet Surrender

"Overtime?" Jackie said. She directed her question toward a stunned Hammer leader.

Braedon glanced over at the half-buried Keegan, who quickly shook his head no.

Drake had already dropped his stick and was doubled over with both hands clutching his knees, still gasping for breath. "I can't move," he said.

Nick struggled to his feet, while Justin and Dax stepped back onto the ice. "Let's keep playing," he said, and pointed to the blades of his skates. "I'm just starting to figure out how these toe-picky things work."

Corey skated over to Jackie, took off his gloves and extended his right hand. "My teammates don't want to play any more because they know you would beat us," he said. "Nice game."

Braedon's shoulders dropped, and he joined Corey in shaking Jackie's hand. "Inlet does have some really good hockey players," he said. "Congratulations."

It was a humble Keegan who made his way toward the rink, still brushing the snow from his uniform and shaking his head. "I can't believe we were almost beat by two guys and a girl," he said.

Jackie cleared her throat. "Excuse me?" she said, as Holland removed her helmet, revealing long brown hair that dropped down to her shoulders. "I'd like all of you to meet my friend, Holly Miracle."

"What?" Keegan said. "Where did you learn to play so well?"

"I'm on a team in Glens Falls," Holly said. "But you're just as good as any boy I've seen in the league there."

Keegan stood a little taller. "I am?" he said. Then he turned to Nick. "Sorry for what I said about your skates."

Nick shrugged. "That's okay," he said. "Actually, I am glad we aren't playing any more today." He sat back down on the ice. "I can hardly feel my toes, and my ankles are killing me."

Justin picked up Dax and listened as the Hammers and Snowcats talked and laughed and in slow motion reenacted some of the more memorable moves and plays. It was hard not to laugh as Nick attempted to take full credit for their team's game-tying goal.

Justin watched with admiration as the ever-generous Jackie hustled to the Snowcat bench and returned with an armful of chocolate hockey pucks, one for each them. "Thanks, Jackie," he said, as she handed him the treat.

"My parents got these in Potsdam," Jackie said. "Hockey is pretty big there, too."

77

"Ice hockey is big everywhere in the Adirondacks," Holly said. "It's one of the best games ever invented."

Braedon took another bite of chocolate. "Hey, Jackie," he said, still chewing. "How would you like to join our team for the youth division of the *Adirondack Ice Bowl*?"

"Thanks," Jackie said. "But I'm thinking now maybe I'll start my own team."

"Then how about a pond hockey rematch next year?" Braedon said.

Keegan chimed in. "And you can come to Old Forge," he said.

"What do you think, Justin?" Jackie said. "Nick?"

Justin and Nick looked at one another and then back at Jackie. "Maybe," they said.

Jackie looked at Braedon and smiled. "That," she said, "would be a yes."

epilogue

Justin picked up the present he bought his parents for Christmas and shook it again. He had loved it from the time he saw it on sale on a bargain table in the summer.

The tiny flakes of snow swirled in the liquid all around inside the globe, quietly settling on the small cabin in the woods. The miniature scene had reminded him of their family camp. He thought his parents would love it, too, and they did.

As the last few chips of white made their peaceful descent, he wondered again if every flake of snow in the entire world was different. Thinking about the hockey game the day before, the thought popped into his mind that people sure were different – so, why not snowflakes, too?

Placing the snow globe back onto its pedestal where it rested on the mantle of the fireplace, he saw something in the miniature scene he had not spotted before. There was the head of a white-tailed deer poking out from behind the branches of an evergreen. He sighed. *Blizzard*, he thought, and he almost wished he hadn't noticed it.

"Justin." It was his mother. The sound of her voice was gentle, but urgent.

"Coming, Mom," he said.

Running from the living room toward the kitchen, his mother intercepted him and put her finger up to her lips. "Shhh." She motioned for him to peek around the corner.

He did.

First, he saw Dax peering out the back window, and he whispered. "What's she staring at?"

"Keep looking," his mom said softly, her hands resting on his shoulders.

Daring to lean out further, what he saw next momentarily stole his breath. "It's Blizzard," he said. "He's all right." Then he smiled. "And he does have a brown patch – a big one, on his left side."

A few flakes of snow appeared and began gently settling on the deer, the trees and the cabin.

Justin had been hoping for a white Christmas.

He got one – and so much more.

 **DAX FACTS**

Highlights of Ice Hockey in the Adirondacks

From amateur ice hockey played on wilderness ponds to professional hockey played in city arenas to international Olympic events at the world's winter sports headquarters in Lake Placid, there is a rich history of this sport on skates in the Adirondacks.

The east end of Fourth Lake near Inlet, NY, is site of the annual Adirondack Ice Bowl featuring amateur hockey clubs from around the world. Portable lights allow continuous action both day and night! *Photos courtesy Adirondack Ice Bowl*

Pond hockey is played in communities throughout the Adirondack Park and was revived on Fourth Lake of the Fulton Chain of Lakes in 2009 with the Adirondack Ice Bowl. Teams now come from around the country and the world to compete in Inlet each year on a long winter weekend.

Ice hockey comes to Inlet, New York. It was in the early 1930s when the Hamilton County Park Commission bought two Canadian hockey teams – one for Speculator and one for Inlet. Fans watched them compete first on the ice of Fourth Lake, and later on an enclosed, inland rink.

One early newspaper report noted, "Ice hockey with its speed and intense fascination has claimed Inlet guests and residents of the Central Adirondacks. Inlet is being represented by a team made up of the best available players of the north country and Canada."

Inlet, NY, has an on-again, off-again history of rugged amateur hockey teams.

Photo at right used by permission Inlet Historical Society. Photo below from Memories of Inlet, *courtesy of North Country Books, Inc., Utica, NY.*

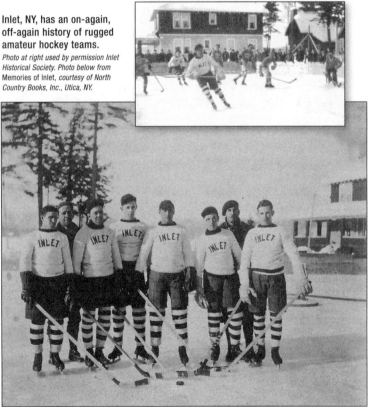

 DAX FACTS

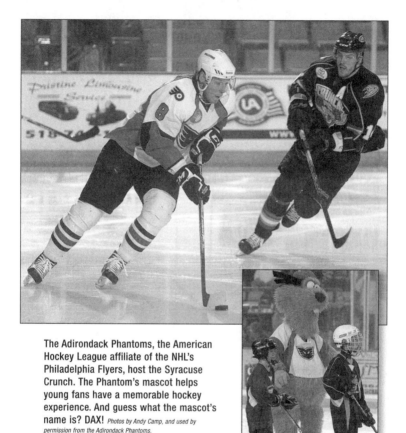

The Adirondack Phantoms, the American Hockey League affiliate of the NHL's Philadelphia Flyers, host the Syracuse Crunch. The Phantom's mascot helps young fans have a memorable hockey experience. And guess what the mascot's name is? DAX! *Photos by Andy Camp, and used by permission from the Adirondack Phantoms.*

The Adirondack Phantoms is one of a number of professional ice hockey teams that has skated its way into the rich history of the Adirondacks. Past teams include the famous Adirondack Red Wings and later the Adirondack Icehawks and Adirondack Frostbite. Teams have been headquartered at the Glens Falls Civic Center in Glens Falls, New York, which has also been home to the Adirondack Hockey Museum.

Team USA celebrates their miraculous victory over the powerful Soviet Union team in the 1980 Winter Olympic Games in Lake Placid, NY. The team later won the Gold Medal in one of the most inspiring Olympic stories ever. *Photo used by permission Lake Placid Olympic Museum*

The legendary Miracle on Ice men's hockey game was played in Lake Placid, New York. It was on February 22, 1980 when TEAM USA comprised of amateur and college athletes defeated a team from the Soviet Union, believed at the time to be the best men's ice hockey team in the world. TEAM USA's 4-3 victory was considered to be a miracle. TEAM USA went on to defeat Finland to win the Olympic Gold Medal. In 2008, the International Ice Hockey Federation (IIHF) selected the United States victory over the Soviet Union as the top international hockey story of the century!

The Lake Placid Olympic Museum is a destination for thousands from around the world to relive the sights and sounds of both the 1932 and 1980 Winter Olympic Games.

 **DAX FACTS**

Albino and Piebald Deer

Albino deer are extremely rare. In an article entitled, *White Deer Seen in Adirondacks*, published in the *New York Times* newspaper more than one hundred years ago, it was noted the unique animal was viewed by many with caution. The superstitious refused to harm a white deer, referred to by many woodsmen at the time as the ghost deer, which they said "flitted ghost-like through the thickets of the Adirondacks." Rodney West, an Essex County woodsman, was quoted as saying, "White deer are rarely seen in the Winter, as they are so nearly the color of the snow and are practically invisible to all but the sharpest eye…" Deer that were all white were reported in

Albino White Tail deer. *iStockphoto. © Neal Warren, Design and Image Studios*

such Adirondack locations as Keene Valley and the regions of Cranberry Lake and Indian River. (*from White Deer Seen in Adirondacks: Regarded with Great Suspicion by the Guides and Natives – No Hunter Will Kill Them, New York Times, July 19,1903*)

Piebald deer are colored white and brown similar to a pinto pony. *Photo © 2012 Eric Dresser*

The piebald deer is also rare, but has been spotted in the Adirondacks recently, such as this one photographed north of the town of Ohio by master wildlife photographer, Eric Dresser. Piebald means "of different colors", and because of a genetic defect, piebald deer are colored white and brown. Sometimes a pie-bald deer can be almost completely white.

 **DAX FACTS**

Snowflakes

Is every snowflake different?
Snowflake Bentley thought so!
Mr. Wilson A. Bentley (1865–1931) is most famous for photographing thousands of snowflakes during his lifetime. In 1885, he became the first person to ever photograph a snow crystal, and he never found any two alike. The Jericho Historical Society of Jericho, Vermont, was established in 1972 and is dedicated to preserving Mr. Bentley's legacy.

A wonderful picture book entitled *Snowflake Bentley* by Jacqueline Briggs Martin with wood block print illustrations by Mary Azarian, won the Caldecott Award in 1999. Shown here are just a few of Mr. Bentley's fascinating photos.

Bentley Snowflake photos courtesy
Jericho Historical Society
and www.snowflakebentley.com

About the Authors

Gary and Justin VanRiper are a father-and-son writing team residing with their family and cat, Dax, in Camden, New York. They spend many summer and autumn days at camp on Fourth Lake in the Adirondacks.

The Adirondack Kids® began as a writing exercise at home when Justin was in third grade. Encouraged after a public reading of the piece at a Parents As Reading Partners (PARP) event at school, the project grew into a middle-reader chapter book series.

The fifth book in the series, *Islands in the Sky*, won the 2005–06 Adirondack Literary Award for Best Children's Book. Books in the series are used in schools throughout the

The Adirondack Kids® writing and illustrating team. From left: Gary, Carol and Justin VanRiper.
Photograph © Adirondack Kids Press, Ltd.

state of New York and titles also regularly appear on the New York State Charlotte Award's Suggested Reading List. More than 100,000 of *The Adirondack Kids®* books have been sold.

The authors often visit elementary schools, libraries and conferences to encourage students to read and inspire them to write.

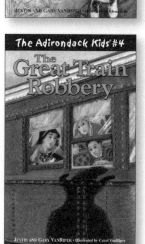

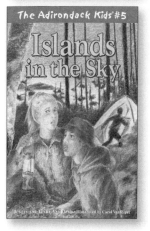

arc found.

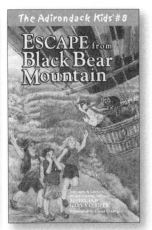

*Watch for more
adventures of
The Adirondack Kids®
coming
soon.*

w.**ADIRONDACKKIDS**.com
ures of The Adirondack Kids® coming soon.